© 1983 by Inga Moore.
First published in Great Britain in 1983 by Andersen Press Ltd.,
19–21 Conway Street, London W.1. Published in Australia by Hutchinson Group
(Australia) Pty. Ltd., Richmond, Victoria 3121. All rights reserved.
Printed in Italy by Grafiche AZ, Verona.
Phototypeset by Tradespools Ltd., Frome, Somerset.

British Library Cataloguing in Publication Data
Moore, Inga
    The vegetable thieves.
    I. Title
    823'.914[J]   PZ7
    ISBN 0-86264-047-4

THE VEGETABLE THIEVES

INGA MOORE

Andersen Press · London
Hutchinson of Australia

Des and Letty had a market garden full of enormous vegetables. Letty was especially proud of the sprouts. They fetched high prices in the shops.

There was always lots to do in the market garden. With all the digging in and pulling out, there wasn't much time for anything else. If Des and Letty went to the cinema, they always had to rush home early to do the watering.

There were days when Des and Letty worked so hard they simply fell asleep at the dinner table, snoring for hours amongst the mashed potatoes.

"There must be more to life than this," they'd grumble as they climbed the stairs to bed.

Then one night, thieves came. They disappeared with two of Des and Letty's best cauliflowers. The next night they stole some swedes and a string of onions from the shed.

By the end of the week they'd taken two cauliflowers, six swedes, a string of onions, a sack of potatoes, leeks, parsley and a very large savoy cabbage.

"What a cheek!" fumed Des and Letty. What would be next? So that night they kept a watch in the garden. But as usual they'd had a hard day and soon fell asleep. The thieves came and went unnoticed. Des and Letty woke to find their broad beans gone and thought of all the horrible things they'd like to do to the thieves if they could catch them. Then they saw an empty pod tossed on the path. Further on there was another – and another. In fact, there was a whole trail of them leading out of the gate and down the road.

They found a couple of good thick sticks and set off in hot pursuit.

The bean pods led them into a dingy part of town. Down a street of factories and workshops was a derelict house. One of the windows was dimly lit and a bean pod lay on the front doorstep.

This is it, thought Des and Letty. They crept up to the window and looked through.

The first thing they saw was a candle. It was on a table, and round the candle were some bowls. Above the bowls were faces. Then someone put a big pot on the table and in the pot were Des and Letty's broad beans, done up nicely in leek and parsley sauce!

They burst in with bloodcurdling yells.

"Got you at last!" roared Des, giving the table a mighty whack with his stick. Letty held her stick at the ready, expecting a fight. The thieves just cringed behind their bowls. Letty looked a little harder – they were children!

"Fetch your parents," she shouted sternly. "At once!"

But the children didn't have any. They did have an uncle who used to look after them, but last week he'd run off with a trapeze artist he met at the circus. So they looked after themselves now. It was easy until their pocket money ran out. Then they had to start pinching things – apples from trees, eggs from hen-houses, milk from doorsteps . . .

"Not to mention beans from gardens and onions from sheds!" yelled Des.

But Letty felt rather ashamed of being cross and tried to think of a way to help. Then she had an idea.

Letty's plan was simple. The next day, after school, Rona, Reggie, Ronnie, Sid and Rita came to the market garden, not to steal the vegetables, but to help Des and Letty look after them.

They pulled out the onions, tied up the beans and watered the cabbages.

In return, Letty cooked them a lovely big dinner of pumpkin pie, bean hotpot and steamed strawberry pudding.

Then they went home. They couldn't remember having so much to eat before.

With the extra help in the garden, Des and Letty felt quite sprightly.

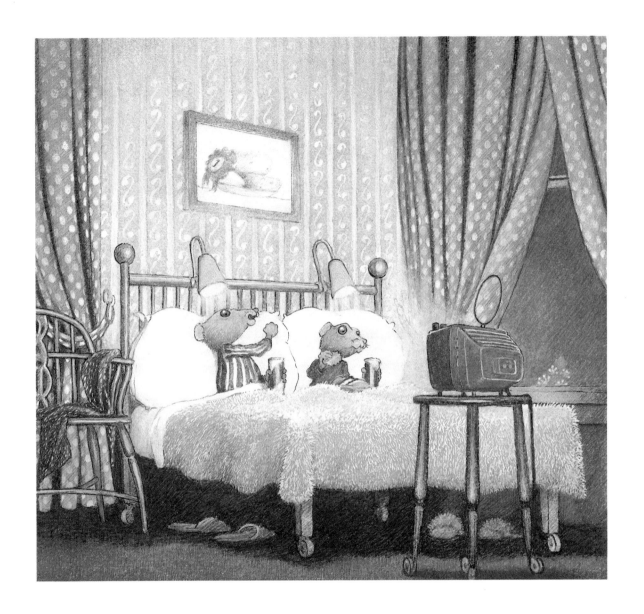

That night they sat up watching television. Not only did they watch a thriller right though, but three different quiz shows as well.

The next day brought a surprise for Des and Letty. Rona, Reggie, Ronnie, Sid and Rita turned up on the doorstep with all their belongings.

"We've come to live with you," they announced.

Des and Letty didn't know what to think. After all they had a very large family now. Just imagine the size of the weekly wash!

But in fact, from that day, life looked up for Des and Letty. With all the children to help with the chores, their work was much easier. Snoring at the dinner table became a thing of the past.

And if you should ever hear a rustling in the beans one evening,
and the whirr of a shuttlecock, you'll know they're out enjoying

themselves with their new family — the day's work done and still plenty of time to play!